OLIVIA™

5-MINUTE STORIES

SIMON SPOTLIGHT

New York   London   Toronto   Sydney   New Delhi

Based on the TV series OLIVIA™ as seen on Nickelodeon™

 SIMON SPOTLIGHT

An imprint of Simon & Schuster Children's Publishing Division

1230 Avenue of the Americas, New York, New York 10020

This Simon Spotlight edition April 2018

OLIVIA Acts Out adapted by Jodie Shepherd, based on the screenplay written by Pat Resnick, illustrated by Patrick Spaziante
OLIVIA™ Ian Falconer Ink Unlimited, Inc. and © 2009 Ian Falconer and Classic Media, LLC

OLIVIA the Ballerina by Farrah McDoogle, illustrated by Patrick Spaziante
OLIVIA™ Ian Falconer Ink Unlimited, Inc. and © 2013 Ian Falconer and Classic Media, LLC

OLIVIA and the Haunted Hotel adapted by Jodie Shepherd, based on the screenplay "OLIVIA Plays Hotel" written by Kate Boutilier and Eryk Casemiro, illustrated by Patrick Spaziante
OLIVIA™ Ian Falconer Ink Unlimited, Inc. and © 2010 Ian Falconer and Classic Media, LLC

OLIVIA the Superhero adapted by Cordelia Evans, illustrated by Patrick Spaziante
OLIVIA™ Ian Falconer Ink Unlimited, Inc. and © 2016 Ian Falconer and Classic Media, LLC

Dinner with OLIVIA adapted by Emily Sollinger, illustrated by Guy Wolek
OLIVIA™ Ian Falconer Ink Unlimited, Inc. and © 2009 Ian Falconer and Classic Media, LLC

OLIVIA and the School Carnival adapted by Tina Gallo, based on the screenplay "OLIVIA Runs a Carnival" written by Joe Purdy, illustrated by Guy Wolek
OLIVIA™ Ian Falconer Ink Unlimited, Inc. and © 2010 Ian Falconer and Classic Media, LLC

I Can Do Anything! by Natalie Shaw
OLIVIA™ Ian Falconer Ink Unlimited, Inc. and © 2016 Ian Falconer and Classic Media, LLC

OLIVIA and Her Alien Brother adapted by Maggie Testa, based on the screenplay written by Jill Gorey and Barbara Herndon, illustrated by Patrick Spaziante
OLIVIA™ Ian Falconer Ink Unlimited, Inc. and © 2014 Ian Falconer and Classic Media, LLC

OLIVIA Leads a Parade adapted by Kama Einhorn, based on the screenplay written by Pat Resnick, illustrated by Shane L. Johnson
OLIVIA™ Ian Falconer Ink Unlimited, Inc. and © 2011 Ian Falconer and Classic Media, LLC

OLIVIA Makes Memories adapted by Lauren Forte, based on the screenplay "Olivia Explores the Attic" written by Joan Considine-Johnson, illustrated by Patrick Spaziante
OLIVIA™ Ian Falconer Ink Unlimited, Inc. and © 2015 Ian Falconer and Classic Media, LLC

OLIVIA Dances for Joy adapted by Natalie Shaw, based on the screenplay written by Madellaine Paxson, illustrated by Patrick Spaziante
OLIVIA™ Ian Falconer Ink Unlimited, Inc. and © 2012 Ian Falconer and Classic Media, LLC

OLIVIA Says Good Night by Gabe Pulliam and Farrah McDoogle, illustrated by Patrick Spaziante
OLIVIA™ Ian Falconer Ink Unlimited, Inc. and © 2011 Ian Falconer and Classic Media, LLC

SIMON SPOTLIGHT and colophon are registered trademarks of Simon & Schuster, Inc.

For information about special discounts for bulk purchases, please contact Simon & Schuster Special Sales at 1-866-506-1949 or business@simonandschuster.com.

Manufactured in China 0218 SCP

10 9 8 7 6 5 4 3 2 1

ISBN 978-1-5344-1163-0

ISBN 978-1-5344-1170-8 (eBook)

These titles were previously published individually by Simon Spotlight with slightly different text and art.

Contents

Olivia Acts Out

"I have some exciting news," announced Olivia's teacher, Mrs. Hoggenmuller. "Our class play this year will be *The Fairy Queen*."

"And *I* will play the Fairy Queen," Olivia whispered to her friend Julian.

Mrs. Hoggenmuller continued, "The Fairy Queen will be played by . . . Francine."

"I bet I get the second-biggest part," whispered Olivia.

"I hope *I* get to work the curtains," Julian whispered back. "That way no one will see me."

"And the littlest fairy will be played by . . . Alexandra," the teacher continued.

Soon there were only two roles left to assign . . . and only two students waiting to find out their roles: Olivia and Julian! Julian was chosen to be Tree Number Three. He had no speaking lines at all.

"Awesome!" he shouted.

"And, Olivia," Mrs. Hoggenmuller finished, "you are Cow Number Two."

At home Olivia complained to her family. "My part doesn't even have a name."

"Of course it does," said her mother. "You're Cow Number Two. Now tell us what you say."

"*Moo*," Olivia answered.

"And . . . ?" her mother said encouragingly.

"That's it," Olivia replied in a grumpy voice. "Only *moo*."

"Well," said her father, "just remember: It's not *what* you say; it's *how* you say it."

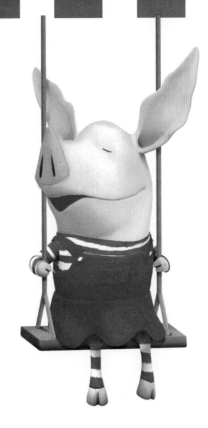

So Olivia practiced saying it all different ways. She moo-ed high . . . and low.

She moo-ed LOUD . . . and soft.

At school the next day the class practiced the show.

It was a disaster!

Harold kept facing the wrong direction.

Julian was allergic to his tree costume. He sneezed loudly every time Francine tried to recite her lines.

"I cannot work under these conditions!" Francine moaned.

"I can!" Olivia volunteered.

Mrs. Hoggenmuller clapped her hands. "Class! Let's take it from the top."

"From the top of what?" asked Francine, puzzled.

Mrs. Hoggenmuller sighed. "That means start at the beginning."

So Francine repeated her line to Cow Number Two, and Julian managed not to sneeze. But Cow Number Two wasn't paying attention. . . .

Olivia imagines the night of the play. Francine is onstage,
looking out at the beautifully dressed audience. She opens her
mouth, but nothing comes out—not even a tiny squeak.

"Oh no!" wails Mrs. Hoggenmuller. "Francine has stage fright! The play will be ruined!"

"Don't worry," Olivia reassures her. "I know every line and every gesture."

She takes center stage. A star is born!

And then Olivia remembered she *was* onstage, as Cow Number Two.

Francine was saying, "For all your good deeds, Little Fairy—"

"*Mooo!*" interrupted Olivia.

Francine tried again. "Little Fairy, you have earned these fairy win—"

"*Mooo!*" Olivia said louder. "*MOOO!*"

"Olivia," Mrs. Hoggenmuller said sternly, "there's not a single *moo* in the script here."

"But, Mrs. Hoggenmuller," Olivia protested, "I think the cow would be happy for the Little Fairy. She would definitely *moo*. She would tap dance, too. Like this."

Back at home, Olivia asked Ian to practice lines with her. But he just laughed. "All you say is *moo*! How much practice do you need?"

"It's not *what* you say, Ian; it's *how* you say it." Olivia tried to imagine herself in the spotlight, stealing the show as Cow Number Two. "Hmm," she said. "What have cows ever done that's interesting?"

"Well," Julian replied, "there's that one cow that jumped over the moon. You know, 'Hey, diddle diddle, the cat and the fiddle . . .'"

"That's it!" exclaimed Olivia. "If you're stuck being a cow, it's good to have a moon to jump over."

The big night finally arrived. Everyone was in place onstage, and the curtain went up. . . .

"I am—" Francine began, then froze. It was just like Olivia's dream!

Uh-oh, Olivia thought. *Francine needs help!* Olivia whispered to her, "I am the Queen of the Fairies."

Those words were just enough to get Francine started. "I am the Queen of the Fairies," she said grandly, and the show began.

Before long, the play was ending. Olivia's big moment was coming.

"You, Horse, will you be merry? And, you, Tree, will you be merry? And, you, Cow, will you be merry?" Francine asked.

"MOOOOOOOOOOOO!" answered Olivia. She leaped up, up, up over the moon, then down, down, down, and side to side . . .

. . . until she landed back on the stage. She grabbed Francine's hand and exclaimed, "THE END!" The cast bowed, and the audience applauded wildly.

Back at home, Mother peeked into Olivia's room, ready to tuck her in. But Olivia was already sound asleep, moo-ing under her breath as she dreamed of jumping over the moon.

So Mother just pulled up the covers and whispered, "Good night, Olivia."

Olivia the Ballerina

Olivia and the other ballerinas in her class were lined up at the ballet barre, carefully practicing their pliés. It was time for Miss Melanie to recite the motto of the famous prima ballerina Penelope Twinkletoes, just like she did at the end of every class:

"The secret to becoming a wonderful ballerina is to eat, sleep, and dream ballet."

"I wish I could spend the entire day at ballet class!" Olivia told Francine. "You know what would be even better? Ballet class all day, every day!"

"Oh, I don't know," replied Francine. "I love ballet too, but think of all the other fun stuff you wouldn't get to do!"

Olivia couldn't imagine anything she would rather be doing than ballet! She decided it was time to take Penelope Twinkletoes's motto more seriously.

"In order to become a prima ballerina like Penelope Twinkletoes, I have to eat, sleep, and dream ballet. That means I can't ever stop thinking about ballet from now on," Olivia told her mom later that day.

"Okay, Olivia," replied her mother. "But can you start after you've taken William out for a walk? He's getting a little fussy, and he needs a walk before his nap."

Olivia decided there was no reason why she couldn't do both things at once: take William for a walk and think about ballet! So after tucking William into his stroller, Olivia took him for a very special ballet walk down the street.

"One, two, three steps on my tippy toes . . ."

"And stop and plié . . ."

"Olivia, what took you so long?" asked Mother when Olivia returned home a while later.

"Sorry, Mom, but I had to practice walking on my tippy toes," Olivia explained. "Plus I had to stop to do a plié after every three steps. But it was worth it because I never once stopped thinking about ballet the whole time!"

That night at dinner, Olivia had a wonderful idea!

"Let's speak French at the table tonight," Olivia told her family. "Penelope Twinkletoes speaks French, so if I speak French too, then I will be thinking like a real prima ballerina!"

Father decided to give it a try. He cleared his throat and said, *"Passez-moi le meat loaf, s'il vous plaît!"*

"You like meat loaf?" Ian asked, scratching his head.

"You want gravy for your meat loaf?" Olivia guessed.

Father explained that he asked them to "Please pass the meat loaf!"

Olivia frowned. This was not going according to plan at all.

The next day at school, Mrs. Hoggenmuller read a story to the class. "Once upon a time, there was a boy who had magic beans," she began.

"Excuse me?" Olivia asked, raising her hand. "Is this story about ballet?"

"No, Olivia," replied Mrs. Hoggenmuller. "This is a story about a boy and magic beans."

As Mrs. Hoggenmuller continued reading, Olivia began thinking about ballet anyway.

". . . and they lived happily ever after!" said Mrs. Hoggenmuller as she closed the book. "Now for homework tonight, please think about the three things you liked best about this story. We will talk about it tomorrow."

Then the bell rang and school was over for the day. It was time for soccer. Today Olivia's team would be playing against the Webster School Wallabies, their biggest soccer rivals.

"C'mon, Olivia," said Francine. "You're goalie today! You get to wear the red jersey!"

Whoosh! A ball zoomed toward the net. Olivia dived for it and caught it. Her teammates cheered. Olivia really loved being goalie. But then she realized she wasn't thinking about ballet!

Then she had a brilliant idea. Instead of diving to catch the ball, she would practice her ballet leaps. Olivia stood in first position waiting for the next ball to head for the goal. She didn't have to wait very long . . . soon a ball came zooming toward her. Olivia raised her arms over her head and gracefully leaped toward the ball . . . and missed it.

For the rest of the game, Olivia missed every single shot. The other team scored ten goals and won the game.

The next day at school, Olivia apologized to her teammates for not doing a great job as goalie. They understood, telling her that everyone has a bad game sometimes, but Olivia still felt bad about letting her team down.

"Okay, class," said Mrs. Hoggenmuller. "Let's talk about the story I read yesterday. Olivia, can you tell me your three favorite parts of the story?"

"Sure," replied Olivia happily. She loved being called on in class. But then she realized that she didn't know what the story was about because she had been daydreaming about ballet.

"Olivia?" repeated Mrs. Hoggenmuller.

"I'm sorry. I don't know," Olivia said sadly.

After class was over, Olivia told Mrs. Hoggenmuller that she was sorry and explained why she was daydreaming about ballet.

"And so, you see, I have to think about ballet all the time if I want to be a famous prima ballerina when I grow up," Olivia finished.

"I don't know about that!" said Mrs. Hoggenmuller. "I wanted to be a teacher when I was your age, but I didn't spend every moment thinking about it! I still did things that had nothing to do with teaching . . . and look at me now!"

Olivia looked carefully at Mrs. Hoggenmuller. She was definitely a teacher! Maybe there was a way to still be a prima ballerina even if she didn't think about ballet all the time. And then she had an idea. A perfect idea . . .

Olivia decided that she would simply wear her ballet outfit all the time! She could wear it while walking William, while paying attention in class, or while playing soccer. She really could wear it anywhere!

"So, Mom, that's why I have to sleep in my tutu," Olivia explained to her mother later that night.

Mother smiled as she pulled the covers up to Olivia's chin.

"Good night, Ballerina Olivia."

Olivia and the Haunted Hotel

"Look at all that rain!" exclaimed Olivia. "Thunder and lightning, too. I love spooky weather!"

"Did you have fun at school today?" asked Mother.

Before anyone could answer there was an enormous *BOOM* of thunder.

Ian and Olivia yelled, "Wooohoo!"

"I know the perfect game to play when we get to my house," said Olivia.

"Welcome to the Hotel Olivia," Olivia greets her guests. "Please come in and make yourselves at home."

"Wow, it's so big!" Francine says.

"This is nothing," answers Olivia. "You should see my other hotels."

Olivia's house made a perfect hotel.

"I'd like a room, please," Francine requested.

"Me too," said Julian. "I mean a different room. Maybe one with a TV."

"Of course," Olivia replied politely.

There was a flash of lightning. *Whooo! Tap, tap, tap.*

The wind whistled and tree branches tapped on the windowpanes.

"What was that sound?" asked Julian nervously.

"Sounds like a ghost," Francine said, trembling.

"Ghost? The Hotel Olivia has no ghosts," Olivia answered firmly. "Follow me, please."

"This is your room, Francine," said Olivia, opening a door.

"No offense, Olivia," said Francine, "but I'd like another room. This one smells like boy."

"I'll take it," said Julian. "I already smell like boy. Does it come with room service?"

"Of course," Olivia answered, opening the door to a second room. "All our rooms do. They also come with fluffy towels and chocolates on the pillows. That's what makes the Hotel Olivia the fanciest hotel in the world."

"I love my new room!" cried Francine. "This is the best hotel ever!"

Brring! A bell rang from downstairs.

"Excuse me," said Olivia. "I think I have another customer."

"I'm sorry, but the Hotel Olivia is completely full," Olivia told Ian.

"No fair," complained Ian. "Mom! Olivia says all the rooms in her hotel are taken."

"Olivia, I'm sure you can find a room for Ian *somewhere* in your large hotel," said Mother.

"This is our last room," Olivia announced. "You'll love the privacy. Plus the soaps are free. But you'll have to leave when the other guests need to use the bathroom."

"Never mind. I don't want to stay at this hotel anyway," said Ian. "Besides, I heard there were ghosts."

"*Ghosts!*" repeated Francine and Julian.

Room service kept Olivia very busy—too busy to play with her brother.

She delivered lunches,

made beds,

cleaned up dog toys,

and soothed frightened guests. "It's just the hotel laundry," reassured Olivia.

That gave Ian an idea.

Suddenly there was a loud bang and everything went dark.

"HEY! WHO TURNED OUT THE LIGHTS?" yelled Francine, alarmed.

"The storm must have knocked the power out," guessed Julian.

"Or a ghost did," whispered Francine.

"I told you, Francine," said Olivia, "there are no ghosts at this hotel."

"BOO!"

"Aah! Ghost!" screamed Francine.

"Aah! I see it too!" screamed Julian.

"Where? There are no ghosts at the Hotel Olivia," Olivia repeated.

Francine and Julian huddled together. "Well, I saw a ghost," said Francine, "and I don't want to stay in this spooky hotel anymore."

"Me neither," Julian agreed. "This hotel is haunted."

HMM. If I do have a ghost in my hotel, then I'm just going to have to get rid of it, Olivia thinks. Good thing I have a Ghost-o-Meter.

"I *knew* it was you, Ian!" said Olivia. Then she called downstairs. "Mom, Ian is scaring my guests."

"Well, Olivia, maybe Ian just wants to play," Mother called back.

"Hmm," said Olivia. "I know! Ian, how would you like to be the room-service waiter?"

"Cool!" said Ian.

"Welcome to breakfast at the ghost-free Hotel Olivia," said Ian the next morning. "Today we are serving our world-famous pancakes."

"Yum," said Francine.

"Double yum," said Julian.

"More pancakes, anyone?"
asked Mother.

Olivia the Superhero

"'*Pow! Zap! Crunch!*'" said Olivia. She and her dad were reading a *Super Force United* comic book together.

"'You'll never stop me, Super Force United!'" Dad read in a Dr. Trouble voice.

Baby William shook his rattle, and Dad and Olivia laughed.

"'The superheroes jumped into action,'" Dad continued. But before they could finish the story, William started crying.

"Looks like he dropped his rattle," Olivia said. "Don't worry, William. I'll find it!"

But the rattle was nowhere to be found. *Hmm,* thought Olivia. *I bet I could find it if I were a superhero. . . .*

Olivia imagines using super strength to save William's rattle from Dr. Trouble.

"Dad, I know what happened to William's rattle," Olivia told her father. "A super-villain-bad-guy took it. And the only way to catch a super-villain-bad-guy is to become a superhero-good-guy!"

She dragged her trunk over and pulled out some supplies. In a flash Olivia became Super Thinker, a super smart superhero!

If Olivia was going to catch the rattle stealer, she needed backup. First she called out her window to Francine.

"Do you want to be a superhero?" asked Olivia.

"Sure," said Francine. "I'm super fast. I could be Super Speedy Clown!"

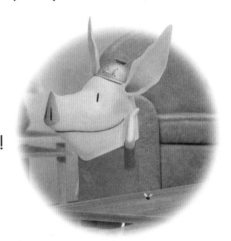

Then Ian demonstrated his super robot hearing skills—he could hear a fly walking across the table!

"Super Robot, you're in!" Olivia declared.

Alexandra wanted to be a superhero too. "I am Super Noisy Dancer!" she said as she did a flamenco dance and clacked her castanets.

"And what's your power, Harold?" Olivia asked.

"I've got a sandwich," Harold replied.

"A super *stinky* sandwich," squealed Alexandra.

"Your name can be Super Stinky Sandwich Man!" Olivia said.

"I hereby call our superhero team The Mighty Five!" said Olivia. "Now, the first thing we need to do is find William's rattle. Super Robot, use your super ears!"

Ian concentrated. "Super Robot detects rattling noises coming from in there," he said.

"The evil rattle thief must be hiding inside!" said Alexandra.

"How do we get him out?" asked Francine.

"Super Stinky Sandwich Man, use your super stinky power!" said Olivia. "Throw your sandwich in the doghouse. Then we'll grab the evil rattle thief when he tries to run away from the smell."

Harold took one last bite of his smelly sandwich and tossed it into the doghouse. The rattling noise stopped, and out ran . . . Perry!

"Are you the evil rattle thief?" Olivia asked her dog. Then she noticed the box of dog biscuits he was holding.

"That was making the rattling sound!" said Alexandra.

"I guess Perry's not our thief," said Francine.

"Finding William's rattle is hard, even for superheroes," Olivia mused. "Mighty Five—we need to split up!"

So Harold and Alexandra went in one direction to find the evil rattle thief, and Ian and Francine followed Olivia in the other direction.

"Keep your ears open, Super Robot," Olivia said to Ian as they snuck around their backyard stage. "That rattle could be anywhere."

Then they stopped suddenly. There was a rattling coming from the stage!

"Mighty Five—I mean, Mighty Three, away!" said Olivia.

But when they leaped out from behind the stage to catch the evil rattle thief, they immediately collided with . . .

. . . Alexandra and Harold!

"Super sorry, super friends," said Olivia. "We thought we heard the rattle."

"You heard my castanets," Alexandra explained. "I was practicing my super loud super powers."

"The rattle is still missing," said Harold.

"Yes, but my super thinking powers are giving me another super idea," Olivia said. "Alexandra can rattle her castanets super loud, and—"

"The thief will think it's a rattle and come looking for it!" exclaimed Francine.

"He'll walk right into our trap," said Ian.

Alexandra began playing her castanets loudly while the rest of The Mighty Five hid. Soon Francine's cat, Gwendolyn, approached the stage. But when Alexandra stopped clicking her castanets, Gwendolyn wandered away.

"Keep playing, Alexandra," Olivia whispered loudly. Sure enough, when Alexandra started to play again, Gwendolyn came back onstage.

Olivia gasped. "Gwendolyn is the rattle thief!"

Olivia and Francine sprang out of hiding to catch Gwendolyn. Francine tried to use her super speed, but Gwendolyn was too fast! The cat bolted away into Francine's house.

The Mighty Five raced after Gwendolyn into the dining room, but there was no sign of her. Then a familiar rattling noise sounded out from under the table. The Mighty Five surrounded the table and pulled out the chairs.

Olivia reached under the table and scooped up Gwendolyn, who had William's rattle in her mouth. "I guess Dr. Trouble isn't the only one who likes noisy toys."

"Sorry, Olivia," said Francine. "I never knew Gwendolyn was such a criminal mastermind."

"That's okay," said Olivia. "The day is saved, thanks to The Mighty Five!"

That night Olivia was happy to give William back his rattle. "Safe and sound, courtesy of The Mighty Five!" she said.

"Come on, Super Thinker," said Dad, chuckling. "It's your bedtime too." He led her back to her room.

"But, Dad, I can't go to bed," Olivia pleaded. "Crime never sleeps!"

"But little girls do," Dad said, tucking her in. "Sleep tight, my little superhero."

Dinner with Olivia

After a busy morning at school, it was finally time for lunch. Olivia joined her friends Julian and Francine in the cafeteria.

"A cream cheese, pickle, and raisin sandwich!" Olivia announced as she opened her lunch box. She took a big bite and smiled.

Julian had a peanut butter calzone for lunch. "Want a taste?" he asked.

"I don't think so," said Olivia.

"No, thank you," said Francine as she took her lunch out of her backpack. It was in a shiny purple box.

"What kind of lunch box is *that*?" asked Olivia.

"It's called a bento box," said Francine. "My parents got it for me in Japan!"

Each compartment held a different kind of food: chicken satay, baby corn, star fruit . . . and that wasn't all. "Look at this!" Francine said proudly as she took her utensil out of the box.

"Wow," Olivia and Julian said at the same time.

"Cool spoon," said Julian.

"Cool fork!" said Olivia.

"It's both—it's a spork!" said Francine. Olivia and Julian were amazed.

Francine dug the spork into her bento box and pulled out a Brussels sprout. "And this is a Brussels sprout. It's from Belgium . . . in Europe!"

"You *like* Brussels sprouts?" asked Julian.

"They're delicious!" Francine answered. "At my house, everything is perfectly delicious!"

Then Francine had an idea. "Olivia, you simply *must* come to my house for dinner!"

"Really? Will there be Brussels sprouts?" Olivia asked.

"Of course not!" said Francine. "We never eat the same food twice in one year."

Olivia was happy to hear that. "I'd love to come. Thank you."

"Perfect!" said Francine. "I'll have my mother call your mother."

At home that night, Olivia decided she needed to practice her manners before going to Francine's house for dinner, so she hosted her own dinner party. She reminded her guests to always say "please" and "thank you" and to put their napkins on their laps. She told them never to fall asleep at the table. She made sure they remembered to chew with their mouths closed.

"At a fancy dinner party, everything needs to be perfect!" Olivia told her guests.

Olivia imagines what dinner at Francine's house will be like. She pictures a fancy party at a mansion in the English countryside, with waiters on roller skates serving pink lemonade in tall glasses with curlicue straws and monkeys juggling fruit . . .

"Olivia! Dinnertime!" called her mother, interrupting her daydream.

At the dinner table, Olivia's brother Ian slurped his spaghetti, splattering her dress with tomato sauce.

One of his meatballs fell to the floor, where Perry, the dog, picked it up in his mouth.

"Perry, that's *my* meatball," Ian yelled, chasing him around the table.

Perry gobbled it up . . . with his mouth open . . . leaving tomato sauce everywhere.

"I am quite sure they don't eat like this at Francine's house," Olivia groaned.

The next day, Olivia walked to Francine's house with her mother and brothers.

"Have fun tonight, Olivia," her mother said, "and don't forget to invite Francine to our house for dinner too."

"OUR HOUSE?" said Olivia, horrified. She looked over at her brothers. Ian was blowing bubbles in his juice box and William's face was smeared with jam.

She imagines what dinner at her house would look like to Francine. . . .

"Welcome to our humble . . . cave!"

At Francine's house, Olivia gave Francine's mother a bouquet of flowers.

"Why, thank you, Olivia, but I have a rule about no fresh flowers in the house," said Francine's mother. "They make such a mess when their petals drop!"

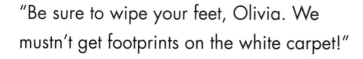

"Be sure to wipe your feet, Olivia. We mustn't get footprints on the white carpet!"

Like any good guest, Olivia told funny stories. Just as Francine's father was telling her it wasn't polite to tell jokes at the dinner table, Olivia saw Francine's mom come out of the kitchen with bowls full of . . .

. . . Brussels sprouts!

Olivia looked at the pile of green in her bowl. To be polite, she decided to take a very small bite. Maybe Francine was right. Maybe Brussels sprouts *were* delicious.

Maybe not.

Olivia quickly reached for her water glass to wash it down but . . . Oops! She knocked one of the Brussels sprouts out of her bowl, and it rolled off the table and onto the white carpet.

Francine's mother and father were not pleased. Olivia and Francine were told to sit at the kids' table.

"Are you mad at me?" asked Francine.

"Why would I be mad?" asked Olivia.

"Because of the Brussels sprouts and the no jokes at the table," replied Francine. "And, well, I was afraid you wouldn't be my friend anymore!"

"Of *course* we're still friends!" replied Olivia. "And you should come to dinner at my house."

Later that week, it was finally Francine's turn to come to Olivia's house for dinner. It was spaghetti night. Again.

"I've never seen anyone do that before," said Francine as she watched Ian slurp his spaghetti.

"Try it!" said Ian.

"I'll race you!" said Olivia.

Turned out, Francine was a natural!

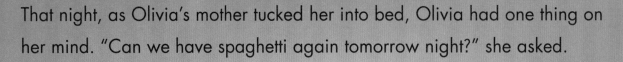

That night, as Olivia's mother tucked her into bed, Olivia had one thing on her mind. "Can we have spaghetti again tomorrow night?" she asked.

"That's a little too soon, don't you think?" said Olivia's mother.

"Okay. Good night, Mom." Olivia yawned.

"Sweet dreams, Olivia," whispered her mother as she turned off the light and closed the door.

Olivia and the School Carnival

"In a few days, our class will be hosting parents' night," said Mrs. Hoggenmuller. "Let's put our thinking caps on and come up with fun activities for the evening. Harold, any ideas?" she asked.

"We can have a finger-painting party! Only you paint with your feet!" he said.

"Thank you, Harold. I will keep that in mind," Mrs. Hoggenmuller said. "Olivia? Do you have an idea?"

"We could make our own carnival!" Olivia said. "We could have games and rides and prizes!"

Olivia's classmates loved her idea. And so did Mrs. Hoggenmuller. "What a fantastic idea," she said. "And, Olivia, I'd love for you to be in charge—with my supervision of course."

Olivia imagines what it would be like to be the ringmaster in a carnival. . . .

"Step right up, everyone, and come see the best, the biggest, the most fun carnival ever made!" Ringmaster Olivia shouts to the excited crowd.

The next day at school, Olivia placed her classmates in groups of three to make up their own booth or game for the carnival.

"How is the Ring Toss game coming along?" Olivia asked Francine's group.

"Oh sorry, Olivia," Francine said. "I decided a ring toss was too boring. So we changed it to a Pin-the-Nose-on-the-Clown game."

"I like it a lot!" Olivia said. "But what if you did something like . . ." Olivia leaned in close and whispered so only Francine could hear.

"What a great idea!" Francine said.

Next, Olivia visited Julian's group.

"We call it the Roly-Twisty Tunnel Ride," Connor explained. "Watch."

Julian crawled inside the tunnel and Connor and Daisy rolled it back and forth across the floor. When the ride was over, Julian could barely stand up straight.

"I'm not so sure about this," Julian said. "It makes you kind of dizzy. Whoa."

"It looks like fun to me!" Olivia said. "But it might be even MORE fun if you tried. . ." And she whispered so only Daisy, Connor, and Julian could hear.

All three of them loved Olivia's idea. They couldn't wait to try it out!

Finally, Olivia checked on Harold's group. She saw a frog sitting in the middle of a bunch of toys. "So your attraction is The World's Largest Frog?" Olivia asked.

"Yes. See how it works? He looks pretty big next to these toys," Alexandra explained.

Before Olivia could say another word, the frog jumped and sat on Harold's head.

"Your attraction is really great," Olivia said. "But I wonder if this might make it even better . . ." She leaned in close to whisper.

"Can you whisper your idea again?" Harold asked. "It's hard to pay attention when there's a frog on your head."

Olivia took the frog off Harold's head and whispered her suggestion right in Harold's ear. He loved it!

When class was over, Mrs. Hoggenmuller spoke to Olivia. "It looks like you're doing an excellent job as carnival director."

"Thank you, Mrs. Hoggenmuller," Olivia replied.

"And how is your own special attraction coming along?" Mrs. Hoggenmuller asked.

"Well, I have lots of ideas, but I haven't decided which one should be my extra special attraction," Olivia said.

Mrs. Hoggenmuller smiled. "Don't worry, dear. Great ideas have a way of sneaking up on you."

On her way home, Olivia imagines she is surrounded by reporters with microphones and cameras. . . .

"Olivia, can we see your extra special, top secret attraction now?" asks one reporter.

"Yes, Olivia, what's under the sheet?" asks another reporter.

"Only the soon-to-be most-talked-about, most-pictures-taken-of, world-famous, most amazing attraction ever built!" Olivia says.

"Show us, Olivia!" begs a third reporter.

"Sorry, but it's not ready for the public yet. You'll have to come back tomorrow, at parents' night," Olivia tells them.

That night, Olivia showed her parents the sketches she had made of her ideas.

Olivia's father looked at all the sketches carefully. "Classic design, very scientific, it pushes, it pulls. . . . You just might need a little help."

Olivia's brother Ian began speaking in a robotic voice. . . .

"Why-don't-you-ask-the-boy-standing-next-to-you?" Ian asked.

"Okay, you can help," Olivia said.

The big night finally arrived. Mrs. Hoggenmuller greeted the parents. "Welcome to parents' night!"

Olivia beamed. "Thank you, Mrs. Hoggenmuller! Folks, follow me to view our first attraction, which was made by Francine, Oscar, and Otto. It's the one, the only, Amazing Clown Beanbag Toss! Would someone care to try it?"

Next, Olivia walked over to what used to be the Roly-Twisty Tunnel Ride. "Here we have Beach Ball Bowling," Olivia announced. "All you have to do is throw a ball through the tunnel and out the other side to knock down these bowling pins! Julian, will you demonstrate?"

Everybody cheered for Julian's strike.

Olivia walked over to the next attraction. "And step this way, ladies and gentlemen, and see The Most Strange Animal of All Time . . . the last living dinosaur, the frogosaurus! Watch it climb up a tall building!"

Harold stood behind a model of the Empire State Building and let the frogosaurus go. It hopped up the building and then right onto his head again!

"And finally, for our last attraction," Olivia said, "welcome to Olivia's Spectacular Fun House!"

Olivia pointed to the fun house behind her. "I couldn't have done it without my little brother Ian!"

Olivia stood in front of the fun house mirrors. "Now watch carefully as the Hall of Mirrors transforms an ordinary boy into . . . The Amazing Robot Boy!"

Ian placed his toy robot in front of the mirrors.

The mirrors made Ian's toy robot look huge! Now it looked like a real robot boy.

All the parents laughed and cheered.

Mrs. Hoggenmuller walked over next to Olivia. "Great job, everyone!" she said. "Parents, enjoy the carnival!"

That night, when her mom tucked her into bed, Olivia was very sleepy, but very happy.

"I really want to show you my idea for a carnival booth," Olivia said.

Olivia's mom smiled. "I would love to look at your idea, Olivia . . . in the morning."

"But my idea glows in the dark, so it's really best if we talk about it now!" Olivia explained.

"Your idea will still be there in the morning. Good night, Olivia."

"Good night, Mom."

I Can Do Anything!

Today was an important day for Olivia. Her dog, Perry, was about to graduate from dog-training school! She helped him practice what he had learned.

"Fetch!" Olivia ordered, and Perry fetched a ball.

"Roll over!" Olivia said, and Perry rolled over. "Good dog, Perry!"

Then Olivia put Perry's leash on him, and he wagged his tail with excitement.

"Perry, heel!" Olivia said as they started walking, and Perry walked calmly without pulling on the leash. "I think you're ready to graduate!" she said, giving him a treat.

At the graduation ceremony, Perry got to wear a special cap.
He looked as proud as Olivia felt.

"You did it, Perry! You graduated!" Olivia patted him on the head.
"I wonder what you'll do next!"

Now that Perry is a graduate, Olivia imagines that he can become a veterinarian who travels the world helping other animals.

"I can see it now . . . ," she thinks. "Dr. Perry will be the best dog doctor in the whole universe!"

That got Olivia thinking. What would she do when she graduated from school? She had liked training Perry, so maybe . . .

Olivia imagines she will be an excellent lion tamer! If she is a lion tamer and Perry is a veterinarian, they can work together in a traveling circus!

"Pleased to meet you!" Olivia will say, teaching lions to shake hands, sit, stay, fetch, and roll over. "Good lion!"

Olivia also liked cooking, so perhaps she would become a chef!

She imagines having her own restaurant, Chez Olivia, where the food will be served on red dishes and people will come from all over to try her famous Super Sparkly Spaghetti!

"Bon appétit!" Olivia imagines saying to her guests.

Then Olivia thought about her favorite hobbies. She loved drawing, painting, and doing anything creative!

Olivia imagines being an artist, creating marble sculptures and painting priceless masterpieces. Maybe one day her artwork will be displayed in a big museum.

Thinking of painting reminded Olivia of another favorite hobby of hers: dancing!

Olivia imagines being a professional ballerina, performing in front of cheering audiences, wearing beautiful costumes, and curtsying to standing ovations every night!

But that wasn't all Olivia wanted to do when she grew up. She liked building model houses with her dad, and she wanted to become an architect, just like him.

Olivia imagines she is a great architect, building houses and skyscrapers and everything in between. And even if blueprints are blue, Olivia will always wear a red hard hat!

Thinking of buildings reminded Olivia of how much she liked to travel and see new places.

She imagines she might like being a pilot with her own red plane someday, as the captain of Olivia Airlines.

"Ready for takeoff!" she will announce to the passengers, then fly into the clouds and land in wonderful destinations all over the world.

But why stop there? Olivia wondered. Thinking about traveling the world made her want to travel to outer space.

"The view is amazing!" Olivia the astronaut will say to Mission Control.

Olivia wanted to be so many things . . . and she kept coming up with ideas, like a star baseball player and a magician.

"How will I ever choose just one thing to be when I grow up?" Olivia asked Perry. "One is just not enough!"

Perry barked and licked her face.

"You're right, Perry. I can do many things!" Olivia decided. "I don't have to pick just one!"

Olivia decided she knew just what she wanted to be when she grew up: She'd be Olivia the pilot/architect/magician/baseball player/ballerina/chef/artist who tames lions in her spare time!

After all, Olivia knew that she could do anything if she believed in herself and worked hard in school. But first she'd have to graduate, just like Perry!

Olivia smiled. There were so many possibilities for her. But for now she was happy to have her imagination . . . and a dog like Perry, even if he misbehaved sometimes!

Olivia and Her Alien Brother

"Look what I made with my pancake," Ian announced one morning at breakfast. "It's a picture of Olivia."

Olivia said, "That doesn't look like me. That looks like a space alien."

"Take me to your leader," replied Ian in his best alien voice.

Olivia began adding her own touches to her pancake portrait. "No great pancake portrait is complete without bows," she explained.

"It's time for you little artists to eat your food," said Olivia's mom.

Ian began blowing bubbles in his milk.

"Mom, are you sure Ian is a member of our family?" Olivia asked.

"Yes, sweetie. I'm positive," her mom replied.

"Because he acts like he's from another planet," added Olivia.

"Another planet?" Olivia's dad chimed in. "I was just reading about a new exhibit at the planetarium. It sounds like it's out of this world!"

"Let's go," Olivia's mom suggested. "We can have a family outing."

After breakfast Olivia and her family piled into the car. Olivia scratched her ears. Ian scratched his ears. Olivia leaned against the front seat. Ian leaned against the front seat.

"Stop it!" Olivia told him.

Olivia's dad had an idea. "Let's see who can be quiet the longest!"

Olivia and Ian both stopped talking, but then they started making faces at each other. Baby William began to cry.

"You made William cry," Ian told Olivia.

"Ha!" said Olivia gleefully. "You talked first."

Soon they arrived at the planetarium. There was so much to see! Olivia and Ian especially loved the glow-in-the-dark planet mobiles.

"If I had glow-in-the-dark planets in my room, I'd probably go to bed early every night, just so I could look at them," Olivia told her mother.

But Olivia's mom shook her head. "No glow-in-the-dark planets today, sweetie."

Olivia sighed. "Well, at least I won't have to go to bed early now, but I sure would like that glow-in-the-dark mobile."

Later Ian looked through the telescope to see if he could spot any planets. "Did you know Pluto is not a planet anymore?" Ian asked his family.

How does Ian know all this? Olivia wondered. *Maybe he's an alien!*

On the ride home, Olivia imagines what Ian the alien looks like.

"Beep, beep, blurg," says Ian the alien.

"Who are you?" Olivia asks him.

"Who are you?" Ian the alien repeats.

"Mom, Ian's an alien from outer space!" cried Olivia.

"It's not polite to call your brother names, sweetheart," replied Olivia's mom.

Back at home Olivia told Julian what she'd discovered about Ian.

"Guess what? Ian is an alien from outer space!" she began. "It's obvious he's studying intelligent life forms on Earth."

Then they heard Ian running toward them.

"Quick, we need to put these on," Olivia instructed, handing Julian a hat made out of tinfoil.

"What are they?" asked Julian.

"Alien mind blockers," answered Olivia. "We don't want him to know what we're thinking."

Ian ran into the room with Perry. They were both wearing metal bowls on their heads. They stared at Olivia and Julian but didn't say anything. Then they left the room.

"See, I told you he's from outer space," said Olivia.

"What about Perry?" asked Julian.

"He's probably using Perry's special doggy hearing to help him communicate with his home planet," Olivia replied.

Julian nodded. "It's all starting to make sense."

Olivia and Julian followed Ian up to his room. Olivia tried peering through the keyhole to see what her alien brother was doing.

"Go away, earthling," Ian said in his alien voice. "Annoying older sisters are not allowed."

"What do you think he's doing in there?" asked Julian.

"Probably building something to rid the world of older sisters," replied Olivia. "I have to find out what that space-alien-pretending-to-be-my-brother is up to!"

So Olivia waited and waited and then waited some more for Ian to come out of his room. Soon it was time for Julian to leave, and still Olivia waited. After a while Olivia fell asleep and Ian finally came out of his room. He was holding a box.

Olivia woke up and began to chase him. "Ian, come back here," she yelled.

"No," said Ian. "It's not ready yet."

"What's not ready yet?" asked Olivia.

As Olivia chases Ian around the house, she imagines that she is an adventurer chasing an alien through outer space.

Space adventurer Olivia dodges asteroids and comets as she follows Ian the alien. Ian the alien zooms away just as the outer space traffic light turns red.

Space adventurer Olivia has to wait as aliens cross the intergalactic highway.

"Please hurry," space adventurer Olivia pleads with them. "My alien brother is getting away."

Soon Olivia had chased Ian all the way back to his room.

She was just about to catch him when she landed on his skateboard and coasted into the closet. Ian closed the door. Olivia was trapped by her space alien brother!

"What do you plan to do with me, space alien?" Olivia called from inside the closet.

"Quiet, earthling, or else," warned Ian.

"Or else what?" asked Olivia.

Ian went into the closet and handed the box to Olivia. "Or else I'll give you this."

Olivia opened the box. "Glow-in-the-dark planets?"

"I made them for you myself," Ian responded.

"Thanks, Ian," said Olivia, and she hugged him. Alien or not, Olivia loved her little brother.

Later that night Olivia's dad hung her
glow-in-the-dark planet mobile from her ceiling.

"Ian's design is really quite inventive.
You have to admire his creativity," he said.

"You're right," Olivia agreed. "Maybe having
an alien for a brother isn't so bad after all."

"Alien?" asked Olivia's dad.

But Olivia was already asleep.

Olivia Leads a Parade

"Ah, nothing like watching a parade from the comfort of your own couch," said Olivia to her dad as they watched a parade on television.

"I want to play that huge drum!" said Julian.

"Look at the floats!" said Ian.

"And the majorettes!" Olivia added. "I'd like to be the one twirling the baton. . . ."

Olivia imagines herself as a marching majorette . . .
spinning her baton . . .
tossing it into the air . . .
twirling around . . .
and doing a split.
TA-DA!

"I wish we could have parades like that in our town," said Ian.

Olivia had a brilliant idea. "Ian, we can have our *own* parade!"

"Great!" said Julian and Ian.

They went right to work. "Julian, you can be the marching band," declared Olivia. "Ian, you can play the cymbals. And I'm the majorette—this ruler is my baton! Now, all together!"

Everyone began to march in place. *BAM, CRASH, BOOM!* went the parade band, and Perry howled along.

Upstairs, Olivia's mother was trying to get Baby William to take his nap. She poked her head out of the window and called down, "Kids, could you play your music a little more quietly?"

"Oops. Sorry, Mom," Olivia and Ian said.

They went inside to look for things they could use in a quiet parade. Olivia found an old pennant from a baseball game.

"Pennants are quiet," she said. She started making a pretty new pennant from the old one.

"Just needs a little glue," she said. "Perfect!"

But the glue stuck to Olivia's hand. "Uh-oh! It's stuck!" she said, and they all giggled.

Olivia ran into William's room, where her mom was still trying to get William to fall asleep.

"Mom, I need a little help!" Olivia said loudly.

William cried loudly.

"Olivia, I asked you to keep the noise down." Her mother sighed.

Olivia, Ian, and Julian went outside to try again.

"Okay, let's take it from the top!" Olivia announced. "Shhh, the cymbals are too loud, Ian. But can you do tricks on your tricycle? Okay, parade, get ready to march! One, two, three, go!"

The three marched along proudly until Olivia's baton got stuck in the tree. Then Ian crashed his tricycle loudly into the garbage cans. This parade was not very quiet.

Just then Francine and Alexandra came by. "What's making all that noise?" asked Francine.

"Shhh!" said Olivia. "Hi, Francine. Hi, Alexandra," she whispered. "We need to be quiet because my baby brother is trying to nap."

"What are you guys doing?" asked Alexandra.

"We're having a parade," said Julian. "Want to be in it?"

Francine seemed interested. "What kind of parade?"

"A fabulous parade," Olivia promised. "But we have to be very quiet."

"The parade will begin here," Olivia explained. "I'll be in the front twirling my baton. Julian will be leading the drummers here. Ian, you'll ride your tricycle here. Francine and Alexandra, you can pull the float back here."

Francine paused. "I think the parade should have clowns in it." She added a clown to the drawing.

"I'm not really a clown person," Olivia told Francine.

"Really?" Francine said. "Well, I'm a clown person! I'll lead my own parade. *With* clowns. Come on, Alexandra." And they left.

"Don't worry—our parade will be much better," Olivia reassured Julian and Ian.

Soon Olivia's mom came to say hello. William was wide-awake and squirmy. "How are you kids doing?" she asked.

"Great," said Olivia. "Mom, you should take William for a drive," she suggested. "He always falls asleep in the car."

"I wish I could," her mom said. "But I have too much work to catch up on. And besides, I wouldn't want to miss the parade."

"Okay, let's decorate the float!" Olivia exclaimed. Francine and her friends decorated their float too, and Francine got into her clown costume.

Both parades marched along the sidewalk until they bumped right into each other.

"Excuse me, Olivia," Francine said. "My parade needs to get through."

"But we thought of the parade first," Olivia pointed out. Then she had an idea.

Olivia imagines a fabulous parade with all her friends. Wouldn't one big parade be better than two medium-size parades?

"Come on—let's join parades!" Olivia said to Francine.

Francine thought about it and talked to her friends. "Okay," she agreed. "But I'm not changing out of my clown costume."

"Okay, follow my lead, everybody!" said Olivia.

Several people had already gathered on the sidewalk to watch the parade.

"Let the parade begin!" Olivia exclaimed loudly. Then she saw her mom holding William.

"I have an idea! Can William ride in the parade too?" she asked her mom.

Her mom smiled and shrugged. "Why not? He's not sleeping anyway!"

Now Olivia was ready.

It was a very noisy parade.

William fell asleep right away.

"Thank you for getting William to sleep today," Olivia's mom said as she tucked her in. "It was a great parade."

Olivia yawned. "I think I'm only going to have a parade once every five years because they're so much work," she said sleepily. "No books tonight, Mom."

"Wow, you must really be tired," her mom said.

"I'll have double books tomorrow," Olivia reassured her. "Good night."

"Good night, Olivia."

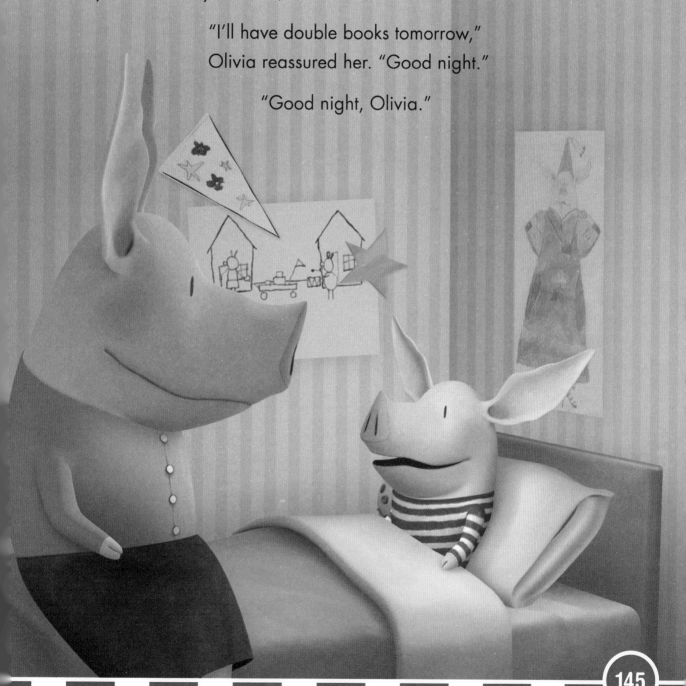

Olivia Makes Memories

One afternoon, Olivia and her grandmother were lying on the grass, looking up at the clouds in the sky.

"Look, Grandma. That one looks like a genie coming out of a bottle," Olivia said. "And over there is an elephant in a tutu."

"You're right, Olivia. That one right there looks like my old steamer trunk," Grandma added.

"Was your trunk like mine?" asked Olivia.

"Yes, it was, but I used it for a time capsule," Grandma replied.

"A time capsule?" asked Olivia. "What's that?"

"Well, people pick things from the time they are living in, and they put them away in a box or a trunk. Years later they open it up to see how much things have changed," explained Grandma. "I made my time capsule when I was just about your age."

"Where is your time capsule now?" Olivia asked.

Grandma shook her head. "I don't know, but I'm sure it's around somewhere."

"Come on, Ian!" said Olivia. "Let's go find Grandma's steamer trunk!"

If I were Grandma's time capsule where would I be? Olivia wondered.

Olivia and Ian explored everywhere they could think of in the house.

"It's not in William's room," announced Olivia.

"The time capsule is not in the bathroom, either," added Ian.

Olivia and Ian crawled through the living room and took a peek under the couch.

"Nice to see you kids playing together," Dad said.

Next, they went into the kitchen and Olivia checked all around.

"Olivia, what are you doing?" Mom asked.

"I'm looking for Grandma's time capsule," Olivia replied.

"I can assure you it's definitely not there," Mom said.

Olivia was frustrated. "Grandma said her time capsule has to be here somewhere, since this house used to be her house."

"We've looked everywhere," Ian said.

"Everywhere except . . . the attic!" Olivia announced.

In the attic, Olivia started opening up all the different boxes and looking inside them.

"I wish I had a map to help me find the time capsule," she said.

Olivia imagines that she and Ian are off exploring a faraway land. They have a map that will lead them to an old and secret buried treasure.

"The map says the treasure is right here," Olivia declares.

She and Ian gaze around in the shadowy stone room. Then they both see the dusty, old trunk in the corner at the same time.

"Aha! The treasure!" Olivia shouts.

Ian sneezes.

"This is it! We found Grandma's time capsule!" cried Olivia. She and Ian opened the trunk and began to look at the things their grandmother had put inside when she was young girl.

Olivia held up a black round disc.

"What is that?" asked Ian.

"I'm not sure," Olivia answered, "but it could go with this." She put the black disc on a machine, turned it on, and music came out.

"Whoa! Cool!" Ian said as he started dancing.

Olivia found a red-striped Hula-Hoop, and then she saw some clothes near the bottom.

"Is this what Grandma wore?" she asked.

She found an old framed picture of her grandmother wearing the very same clothes!

"I guess so!" Olivia was excited.

"Grandma, we found your time capsule in the attic!" Olivia said. She was dressed up in her grandmother's old clothes and she was Hula-Hooping like a champ.

"Mother, you wore that stuff?" Olivia's mom asked.

"Of course," said Grandma. "And I was pretty good with the hoop in my day."

"Want to give it a try now, Grandma?" asked Olivia.

Grandma took the Hula-Hoop from Olivia and put it around her own waist.

"I've still got it. Hula! Hula! Hula!" Grandma chanted.

"I'm glad I found your time capsule, Grandma," said Olivia. "If I hadn't, I might have never known all this about you."

"It's good for families to learn new things about one another and then remember those things," Grandma explained. "Now that you helped me remember *me* as a little girl, I hope I'll always remember you as a little girl."

Olivia had an idea. "I'll make my own time capsule."

"Great idea. So, what should we put in it?" Grandma asked.

Olivia went through her closet and pulled out one of her dresses.

Next, Grandma and Olivia searched through the yard.

Grandma held up a bat. "How about this?"

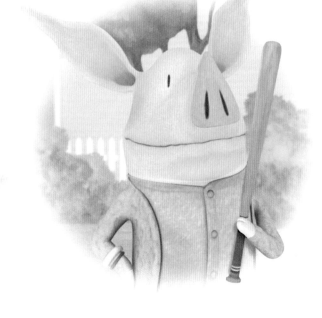

Olivia shook her head.

"A yo-yo?" Grandma asked.

"Not quite right," said Olivia.

"I've got it. Your jump rope?"
Grandma asked.

Olivia smiled. "Perfect."

Olivia and Grandma spent the rest of the day looking around the house for other items that Olivia could put into her time capsule. They even found her favorite bow when they took a peek under the couch.

"Nice to see you kids playing together," Dad said.

Olivia chose a few more things to put in her trunk—even her special sunglasses!

"These are very excellent choices, Olivia," Grandma said. "I think it's just about complete."

"I feel like it needs just one more thing," Olivia said as she looked around the attic.

"The camera from my time capsule still has film in it," Grandma said.

"What's film?" asked Olivia.

"I'll show you," answered Grandma, and she held out the camera, clicked a button, and a piece of paper came out of it.

"One more," Grandma said and clicked the button again. "These pictures will be ready in a jiffy. Two minutes tops."

Olivia was shocked. "You had to wait two whole minutes to see your pictures when you were a girl?"

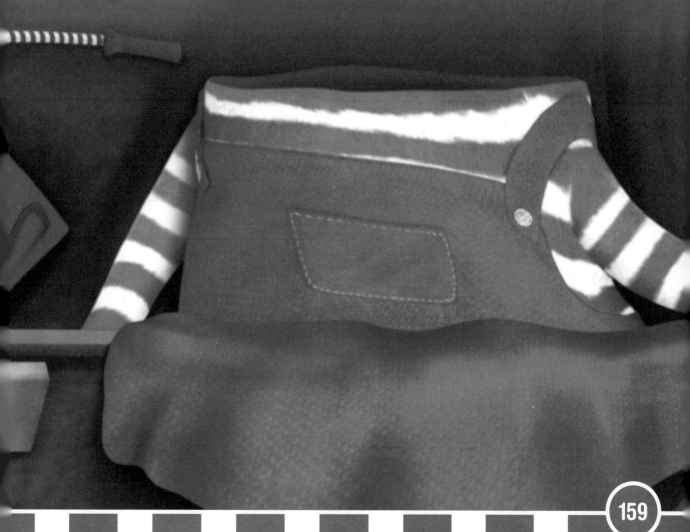

As Olivia watched the paper, a picture of her and her grandmother appeared.

"This is what my time capsule was missing!" Olivia said.

"Mine too," replied Grandma.

They put a photo into each of their trunks, and then they hugged.

At nighttime, Grandma tucked Olivia into bed.

"Thank you, Olivia," she said. "It was fun to remember when I was your age."

"This day will be fun to remember too," Olivia said as Grandma gave her a kiss.

"Indeed, it will," Grandma said. "Good night, Olivia."

"Good night, Grandma," Olivia said.

Olivia Dances for Joy

Olivia and her friends were having a great time in Grandma's dance class, as always.

"Show me your happy dance, everyone!" Grandma said. Each of the kids danced across the room, doing their favorite moves.

Ian did the Robot, Julian did the Moonwalk, and Olivia did lots of pirouettes.

After everyone had a turn to dance, Olivia noticed a new poster on the wall. "Who are the dancers?" she asked Grandma. "They sure look like they're having fun!"

"They're The Prancer Dancers! They won last year's Maywood Dance Contest," explained Grandma.

"We should enter this year's contest!" said Olivia. "Maybe we can get our pictures on a poster too!"

Olivia was already thinking about what it would be like. She smiled and said to herself, "I wonder . . ."

Olivia imagines they have just won the Maywood Dance Contest. She takes a bow and poses for the paparazzi.

"Over here, Olivia!" a photographer yells.

"Give us your famous smile!" says another.

She blows a kiss at the photographers and poses for one last picture. Then she hears someone calling her name. . . .

"Hello? Olivia?" Ian asked, waking his sister from her daydream. "Is anybody home?"

"Sorry, I was just thinking about what it would be like to win the dance contest," Olivia said.

"We don't have a chance. The Prancer Dancers always win," Francine insisted, pointing at the team on the poster. "They dance perfectly together all the time."

"That doesn't sound like much fun!" replied Olivia. "How good can those Dancy Prancers be, anyway?"

"They're called The Prancer Dancers, and you can all see them for yourselves at their rehearsal tomorrow," answered Daisy.

The next day at the rehearsal, The Prancer Dancers lived up to their reputation. They did exactly the same dance moves at exactly the same time. They were perfect.

"We're going to get stomped," Otto said. "Sorry, Olivia, but we don't want to lose." He walked out of the room, and Oscar and Alexandra followed him.

Daisy was about to leave too, but Olivia begged her to stay.

"There's nothing you can do to make me stay on the team—" Daisy said.

"What if I name the team 'Daisy's Dancers'?" Olivia interrupted.

"—except that," Daisy finished. "Count me in! But we need nine dancers to enter the contest. Where will we find three more dancers?"

Olivia set off to find more dancers. Suddenly she spotted the mailman running away from a tiny, barking dog. But he wasn't running, exactly. He was zigging and zagging.

"Ha-ha! You think you can catch me?" the mailman shouted.

"That's one dancer," Olivia said to herself.

Soon after, Olivia heard someone beatboxing.
It was Firefighter Fred.

"Oh yeah! Uh-huh!" Firefighter Fred rapped as
he polished the fire truck, pausing to pop and lock.

"That's the second dancer!" Olivia said.

Next, Olivia walked by school and heard a bell ringing. She looked through the classroom window and saw Mrs. Hoggenmuller ringing a cowbell, singing, shimmying, and doing the Locomotion for her live audience . . . the class pets!

"Chugga, chugga, chugga, chugga . . . Choo! Choo!" Mrs. Hoggenmuller said.

"That's the third dancer!" Olivia said.

It was time for the first rehearsal. Daisy tried to teach everyone to do a perfect ballet twirl. Everyone tried to follow along, but Mrs. Hoggenmuller kept doing the Locomotion by mistake and Julian kept bumping into everyone.

"Try not to look so wobbly," said Daisy. "Spin, people!"

Julian tried to spin faster but became so dizzy that he spun out of control and knocked everyone to the ground.

"This is hopeless! None of you can dance alike." Daisy pouted. "Sorry, Olivia, but I quit!"

Grandma had been watching the rehearsal and asked Olivia what was wrong.

"Julian can't spin," Olivia said.

"But he can do the Moonwalk," Grandma replied.

"But Francine can't do the Moonwalk. She can only tap dance," explained Olivia. "We can all dance, but we can't dance the same way. We'll never win."

"Maybe you should try to forget about winning and just dance because it makes you happy!" said Grandma. "Dance for joy!"

"That's it!" Olivia said. She asked Grandma to take Daisy's spot and gave the team a new name: The Joy Dancers!

Finally, it was the night of the big contest. After The Prancer Dancers did their famous dance, it was time for Olivia's team to go.

"Whatever you do, forget about dancing alike. Dance your happiest happy dance ever! And don't forget to have fun!" Olivia whispered to the team.

The music started and Olivia tapped Ian on the shoulder.

"Go, robot; go, robot; go, robot," she chanted. Ian did his best robot dance and the crowd went wild!

"Go, tapper; go, tapper; go, tapper," the team chanted together, and Francine tap-danced across the stage, click-clacking her feet in time to the music.

One by one, the rest of the group did their favorite dances.

Julian did the Moonwalk.

Harold did a country-western dance.

Mrs. Hoggenmuller
did the Locomotion.

The mailman zigzagged
across the stage.

Firefighter Fred did
the pop and lock.

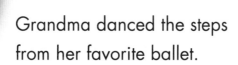

Grandma danced the steps
from her favorite ballet.

Olivia delivered a showstopping finale, doing pirouette after pirouette until the crowd rose to its feet and began to cheer! The Joy Dancers won the contest!

"Come on, Joy Dancers! Smile for the cameras!" Olivia told the team. Daisy even came by to congratulate them.

That night Grandma tucked Olivia into bed. "You really did it!" Grandma said. "You won the contest!"

"You know what, Grandma? I'm happy we won, but I'm even happier that we had fun!" Olivia replied sleepily.

"Good night, my happy little dancer," Grandma whispered.

Olivia fell asleep and dreamed about dancing for joy.

Olivia Says Good Night

One evening, a little while before bedtime, Olivia was reading a story to Ian. It was a wonderful story about a princess who had an adventure in the desert.

"The best part was when they built that beautiful tent," said Olivia as she finished the story.

"That was my favorite part too," agreed Ian. "But there should have been robots!"

Olivia imagines what it would be like to live in a beautiful tent in the desert, just like the princess in the story.

"I wonder . . ."

"Where do you want all this treasure?" Prince Ian asks.

"Over by my dresses, please!" says Princess Olivia.

"Ian, I have an amazing idea!" Olivia said excitedly. Just as Olivia was about to tell Ian her idea, Mom came in.

"It's getting late," she said. "Please start cleaning up and then get ready for bed."

"I guess your amazing idea will have to wait until tomorrow," said Ian.

"No, it won't," replied Olivia. "We're going to build a tent in my room, just like the one in the story! We can clean up and build at the same time!"

"We can?" asked Ian.

Under Olivia's expert direction, they got right to work.

"All right, Ian," said Olivia. "Toys go in the trunk . . . books on the shelf . . . and everything we need for our tent can go on the bed."

Before they knew it, the room was clean!

As Olivia was putting some last things away in her trunk, she saw exactly what she needed to finish the tent.

"Your room looks great," said Ian.

Olivia pulled the blanket from her bed. She draped it to make a flap door, just like on a real tent.

"Hmm . . . it needs one more thing," Olivia noted as she added a glittery red **O** to the flap door.

"Awesome!" exclaimed Ian.

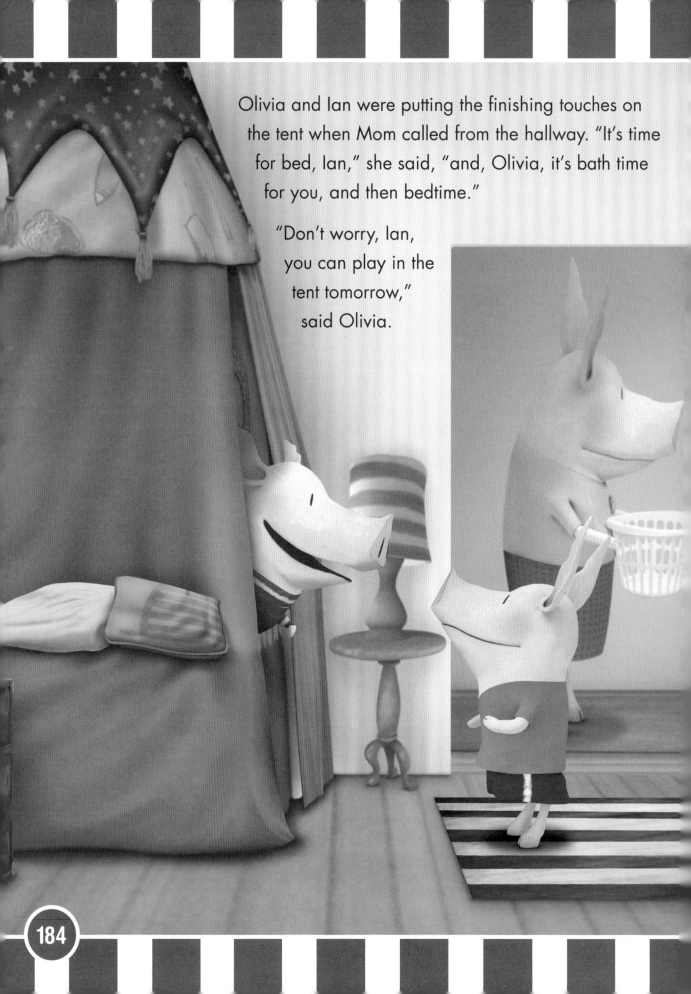

Olivia and Ian were putting the finishing touches on the tent when Mom called from the hallway. "It's time for bed, Ian," she said, "and, Olivia, it's bath time for you, and then bedtime."

"Don't worry, Ian, you can play in the tent tomorrow," said Olivia.

As Olivia settled into her warm and sudsy bath, she remembered that every tent needs treasure, and where better to find treasure than the bottom of the sea?

She imagines what it would be like to be a scuba diver exploring for treasure.

"I wonder . . ."

A pod of seals are all pointing their flippers in the same direction.

"Jewels? Over there?" Olivia asks them, and they nod their heads. "I have a way with animals," Olivia says as she swims that way. And then she spots it . . . a huge treasure chest overflowing with glittering jewels!

"This treasure will be perfect—perfectly perfect!" Olivia thinks happily.

Olivia collected the treasures she had found in the bathtub and took them back to her room. She started to put her treasure away when Mom walked by. She had just finished tucking Ian into bed. "I'll be right there, Olivia," she called. "Don't forget your pajamas!"

"These pajamas are pretty good, but I need something extra special to wear inside my tent," Olivia decided. She remembered the flowing gown the princess in the story had been wearing.

"I know!" Olivia exclaimed. She dug through her trunk until she found what she was looking for . . . the scarf Grandma had given her!

"So glamorous!" she declared.

"All right, Olivia, time for bed!" said Mom when she came into Olivia's room.

"But, Mom, I just finished building the most spectacular, super-duper tent ever!" Olivia protested.

Mom looked around Olivia's room, which was all cleaned up. Then she saw Olivia's tent and was amazed. "That is a beautiful tent," Mom said. "Great job!"

"Ian helped!" Olivia reminded her.

"But it's missing something," said Mom.

"It is?" Olivia exclaimed. *What could possibly be missing?* she wondered.

"Your tent is missing a beautiful girl sleeping inside!" Mom explained.

Olivia settled inside, and Mom tucked her in.

"Good night, Olivia," Mom said.

"But I can't sleep yet!" Olivia said with a yawn. "There's still so much to do. . . ."

Mom smiled and gave her a gentle kiss good night.

When Mom left the room, Olivia sang to herself:

They say "Good night, Olivia.
Your big day is through."
But how can I sleep?
There's still so much to do!

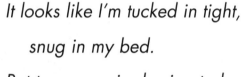

It looks like I'm tucked in tight,
snug in my bed.
But tomorrow is chasing today
through my head.

Will I climb the highest mountaintop?
Or will I paint my masterpiece?
Go ride a bronco in the rodeo?
Or wow the crowd on my trapeze?

Princess, doctor, author, astronaut!
From jungles dark to oceans deep,
I'll do anything, go anywhere.
Just don't ask me to . . .

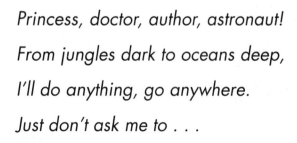